# PART ONE

# 1

I was recently trying to remember the first time I heard his name. I wish I could remember the first time I heard of every person important to me, if only just to know the definitive beginning of every journey I was about to undertake with each one of them. Despite priding myself on having an incredible memory, it was a strangely amusing revelation to myself that I can't quite recall the exact moment anyone came into my life, except for one: *Albert Kaine.*

**1, 2, 3, 4, 5, 6....**

I spent more nights behind bars than I'm proud to admit. Sometimes they were minor violations, sometimes they were far more significant, but I always managed to leave unscathed. That's the luck you get when you know the right people.

That was the beautiful part about being with Lori. She was too good. She was the type of person who would radiate grace and an unparalleled sense of confidence and sympathy. I felt invincible with her. To be loved by other people in a non-romantic fashion isn't necessarily a gift you wish to possess, but I indeed had it, or at least felt it, when I was with her. And in a split second, it ended. I never envisioned it. Maybe I had thought of the possibility of a misfortune ending our relationship, but never that way. To suddenly lose someone in an accident is far more tragic than any other alternative. Every relationship indeed ends in tragedy – be it heartbreak, death, or anything in between – but I still never expected to feel so broken when she was gone. She held me together, to be honest.

At first, it's a unique sadness that consumes you for some months. For me, it exhibited itself in drinking. Drinking later took down my life. I was no longer Roy Hill, but a mere shadow of the man. I had so many rough nights for the first three years that spending a night in a police cell after a fight was a common occurrence and often even better than spending them in my own home. Some nights went by fast, others not so much. Insomniac nights feel longer than dull days. I used to count numbers for hours until I felt a substantial amount of time had passed.

**...98, 99, 100, 101...**

Then, as an almost planned moment of fate, a police officer approached me as I left one morning. He took me to the side. We had shared brief stares before, but I never thought there was a meaning behind them. He was young, clean, and tall, a complete contrast to my physique at that time. "Look for Albert Kaine. Let him show you. Let him," he said, with a strange sense of urgency. He handed me a small presentation card as he left. I thought about the name and how funny it sounded, almost like the names you read in those old books my granny used to have in her library.

I tried ignoring the man's request, although I had to hand it to him – my curiosity was peaked. When you're deep into a depression, any kind of distraction or minor thrill can get your emotions up. The mere oddity of the name Albert Kaine and how he could be of any help to me, at least in the perspective of the officer, was indeed a question I was interested in having answered.

*Little did I know.*

# 2

I was having second thoughts. If he had been suggested to me a few months back, I wouldn't have even considered going. But the idea that the name came into my life just at the right moment when I was planning on changing for the better had to mean something. Plus, my daughter needed me to be better. She would soon be a teenager, which in part meant I had to be more engaged in her life to take care of her. If Mr. Kaine indicated at least an ounce of help, maybe it was worth it. And so I went.

It was a long drive. So long, in fact, that it took me far longer than expected due to the sudden cognizance that I was going farther than I had gone since Lori was gone. Now it sounds ridiculous, but at the moment, it meant something to me to know I hadn't left a certain perimeter in years. I was afraid that leaving that area would say I was taking a step closer into letting her go, and I didn't want to. And yet, I kept going, through tears and sweat.

Not even grief was capable of dealing with my wonder. And so, I arrived.

It was a house, a big one, like the ones that you see in the movies that seem too good to be true. It was big, white, and had a victorian style that, for some reason, still managed to look both hip and classic. I loved it. Lori and I used to love going to affluent neighborhoods and snoop around the houses and marvel at the magnificent architecture on display, wishing to have one ourselves one day. How time flew by so fast is beyond me.

As I approached the door, a man came to me from behind.

"I'm Leo," said the man. "Is there anything I can help you with?"

I looked around. Leo, who had a precise tone that could seem nice to outsiders but was evident hidden condescension to me, waited anxiously for me to respond.

"I'm looking for Albert Kaine."

I took the presentation card out of my pocket. He swiftly grabbed it and examined it from both sides, and as he finished, subtly looked up to me, nodded, and opened the door in silence.

"At the end of the hallway to the right," he said, and quickly went back to the front porch.

The house was, as I correctly predicted from outside, shining clean on the inside, with furniture and ornaments that I deduced could be worth more than I have ever earned in my lifetime. As I passed through the white and gold hallway, I could sense other people were there, but no sounds were made. I remain skeptical to this day if that assessment was accurate.

I turned right. An intimidating maroon door towered over me. I could hear classical music coming from inside. I was about to knock when he opened it. "Welcome. I'm Albert Kaine. I was expecting you, Mr. Hill." His warm and cozy demeanor was instantly palpable. He was tall, thin, bald, and I calculated he was at least fifteen years older than me. My doubts about his age notwithstanding, he wasn't young, but he was the type of man you could tell was well preserved. I suspected he probably looked much cleaner and healthier besides me. He had one of those memorable faces full of cracks and wrinkles, almost like forming a twisted jigsaw.

"Care to join me inside?" he continued. I followed. "How did you know my name?" I asked, genuinely curious by his instant knowledge of me.

"At the risk of sounding disturbing, I had my eyes on you, Mr. Hill." It was disturbing. "You see, I'm starting some kind of movement...or whatever you feel free to call it. I'm looking for different personalities, people willing to become a better version of themselves. I got that sense from you."

Different alarming questions floated in my head. Movement? How did he get that from me?

He stopped me before I even muttered a word.

"I know, I know. It's crazy. The thing is, I've tried to keep an eye everywhere recently, so you're not the only one I've summoned here. This, what I'm starting, is much bigger than you and me, Roy. May I call you Roy?"

"Sure."

"Great. I'm so glad to be having this conversation with you, by the way. I love connecting with people like you."

"Broken people, perhaps?"

"Nonsense. You're not broken. But you're in dire need of reformation, and my gut feeling is that you are aware of it, and that's why you came."

I was getting uncomfortable. He seemed both the most welcome and mysterious person I had ever met. Who was he? How did he know so much about me? What did he get out of me?

I sat back, confused.

"I'm sorry, Mr. Kaine. But I'm not quite sure who you are, what your so-called movement is, or what your deal is. I guess I just expected this to be some kind of therapy or-"

"Oh, but it is, son. It is." He stood up, smiling, almost too excited to contain what he was about to say. "Have you ever heard of The Path?"

I tried to remember. For some reason, it rang a bell. I was just not sure from where.

"Not really, no."

Albert handed me a paper full of text with a nice font. He leaned in.

"You have stumbled into something quite special, son."

...

*THE PATH*

*by Albert Kaine*

**HAVE YOU EVER WONDERED WHAT THE MEANING**

**OF LIFE IS?**

*Of course you have. Without that existential question, we wouldn't have religion, and by design, our world would be much different from what we know today.*

*But breathe in. The answer is far from unattainable. I have studied this question myself for at least the last half of my life. I faced some pretty significant obstacles in my life that brought me to question everything I believed, and instead of giving up altogether, I found myself with a new philosophy; I like to call it The Path. Others might favor to call it The Way, or even The Choice, relating to the significant decision you will make when you determine to embark on this journey with me.*

*Here's the truth about The Path: I believe, my friend, that we, as a human race, are nearing the apocalypse. I have seen it clearly in my visions that if we continue down this path of tribalism, envy, and war, our world as we know it will soon perish and become a mere memory of what once was. Still, it has become clear to me that this prophecy is far from decided, and The Path has chosen me to be the messenger into the world and spread love and compassion all around. One way to do it is to purify the souls of those who have been lost in their path because of a deep desire to find a sense of belonging; in fact, that is precisely how I became interested in you.*

*I am constructing an ideal community, or at least as near as I can get to one, full of people who have been either reformed, purified, restored, or woken up to what The Path has to offer them. If we achieve this goal on a larger scale, I believe we can attain peace on a magnitude that has not been seen for the past centuries. Together, we can save the human race by believing in ourselves and letting The Path show us the right direction.*

On The Path, we do not believe in a higher being or a God; instead, you are your own master, and only you can correct the world order by the high power you have inside that has not been fully realized.

I spend my time traveling around the country (soon the world) spreading my teachings, and when I have the fortune to be here, I like to perfect The Path and find within me discoveries that I can offer. Unfortunately, we have mostly kept The Path a secret to prevent it from ridicule or any possible attempts to undermine us from authorities. Still, with your help and of so many others soon to come, I believe The Path is on its way to become a force to be reckoned with and the clear answer to purify the world.

Join me, my friend.

*-Albert Kaine, founder and Chief Preceptor of The Path*

# 3

A few days after I visited Mr. Kaine in his house, I accepted his job proposal: I would be his main companion in exchange for extensive teachings of The Path to both me and my daughter and permanent residence at his house.

At that time, I was quite unsure what my feelings were regarding The Path. On the one hand, I was never really into any higher philosophy or religion in my life. Still, on the other, there was undoubtedly something genuinely captivating about Albert's dedication to what he had birthed. In a way, I admired it. The feeling of adoration and genuine love that had left from my life when Lori was gone was back when I was with Mr. Kaine. People genuinely adored him, especially everyone inside the house. When I got there, we were roughly about twenty people, but the group quickly grew. It reminded me a lot of my time working at the animal shelter in Denver, where we would regularly see stray animals get in and be in a different shape once they were adopted, only here, they never left. It was a genuinely shocking thing sometimes to see certain people be totally "reformed," as Albert would refer to it.

Some sacrifices had to be made to stay there, but at that moment, they were all mostly minor. We could only leave the house with the Albert as a companion or make a request days in advance. Still, in that town, there wasn't a lot you would need to leave, especially with groceries, healthcare, and school being taken care of (my daughter was being homeschooled by a couple of the Lieutenant Preceptors, which were themselves a married couple of reformed Path-seekers. I felt comfortable with her on their hands.

As for me, my days usually consisted of being a personal assistant for Albert. Sometimes it was as simple as watering some plants. Other times, it was as exciting as accompanying him on a trip. It kept me busy, and, for the first time in quite a while, I felt I belonged somewhere.

It was at night where things got complicated. As part of my Therapy of Reformation, I had to meet with a Preceptor every day at eight o'clock. At first, it was relatively simple: I would sit down and get asked about my life, asked to do some drawings, and sometimes even just talk about what bothered me and my opinions of the place. Afterward, I would be directed to Albert's office to quickly recap my thoughts on the appointment and what I expected from the next day. Fairly simple. By August, I was finally slowly warming up to the idea of The Path, and I was given a choice to level up.

"If you're truly ready to go the next step, I need you to become completely engaged with The Path, Roy," Albert told me, in our usual weekly meeting.

I was ecstatic.

"I'm ready, sir. I feel like I am truly awakening something deeper within me is allowing me to sense The Path much clearer than ever before."

He approached me and handed me a small notebook. "I will need to go on some trips next month. I need you to come with me. I feel it's a good way to get you started on your next step," he said.

"This journal is a gift from me; you deserve it. Feel free to write whatever you want, but I would encourage you to write about our upcoming trips and your thoughts on The Path. That will help you. But still, remember it's completely private, of course. So feel free to write what you please."

And just like that, I was as committed to The Path as I had been to anything else in my entire life, and was indeed excitedly looking forward to what it had for me in store.

# 4

*Journal Entry: 1*

*September 8th*

*Green River, Utah*

*Yesterday, we went fishing. Albert had told me all about how fishing here in Green River evoked memories of the time he spent with his father on vacation. I had never gone fishing myself, but to enjoy the moment with him was indeed a special occasion and could feel the palpable emotions that the activity elicited on him.*

*This is the farthest trip I've taken with Albert, but I think it's safe to say it's my favorite so far. Green River seems more of a touristic site than an actual place to live, but I never expected it to feel so lively and beautiful. In some areas, I even feel like I'm on another planet. The calmness and connection with nature of the place have, I think, helped me link myself with The Path better than ever before. I just wish Lori was here to see it all.*

*We're staying at a modest motel at the outside of the town, and I'm sharing the room with Lee, a new member of The Path who has been assigned to me by Albert to help me out. He's a former drug addict, or so he says, but something about him doesn't scream that to me. In any case, he's becoming a good friend of mine; I think we could truly connect here.*

*Albert has assigned us shorter personal appointments as therapy here as he has no help, but to be frank, I like the more personal approach it provides, even if he isn't entirely sure it works. As I have leveled up, I've noticed minor changes in my therapy; Albert has been more upfront with his questions, and I often feel nervous during the process. Still, I can't say I don't feel purified by the time I'm done.*

*He's told Lee and me several stories of the early days of the foundation of The Path and how he came to convince his wife, children, and even himself of the power and knowledge he held in his mind. He also says he used to have many visions back in the day, usually manifesting in his dreams, but as time has gone by, they have begun to disappear. He has hypothesized that it could be either that he has made so* much progress spreading the teachings that the dire visions he once had are no longer accurate, or that his mind has been acclimating to a much bigger idea he is yet to be ready to confront. I like to believe the former theory, although my more cynical side tells me the latter is quite possible as well.

This morning, we went to the town and met Christy, an older woman, in her home. Albert seemed to know her well, but I felt it was too upfront of my part to ask him outright how he met her. We spent the whole day there. As Albert talked with Christy, he tasked Lee and me to introduce the children in the house to The Path. Some took it seriously while others, I could tell, were making fun of us. Too bad, although I acknowledge my understanding of their feelings as I once found myself in their places. But if I found a way for The Path to become clear to me, I am confident I can do so for them. Maybe that can help me with Albert and even make him consider to fast track my therapy.

A few moments ago, he sat down with Lee and me and talked about the family we had spent the day with, the Pines. Without going into detail of how he came to know them, he did inform us of a new strategy to spread the teachings of

*The Path. As a way of cutting expenses and enabling people of different backgrounds to practice it, he would seek to instruct*

*Area Preceptors in various key cities and towns around the country, and the Pines would be the test subjects of the approach.*

*I like the new strategy. For some reason, despite my months-old acceptance of The Path and its teachings, I'm for the first time fully embracing the magnitude of the movement we are building.*

*How exciting.*

# 5

I felt a thin bright ray of sunshine directed at my left arm. It had been a while since I had appreciated the organic warmth of the sun. I looked in the mirror just before I got out and gently stroked my long, gray beard.

As I walked outside, it was the rocky road hurting my bare feet what I first noticed. Then, it was the ray of sunshine getting wider and feeling it on my face. Even as I struggled with my feet, which were now covered in blood, I couldn't take my eyes off the sun, which was inexplicably growing in size as I walked towards it, as if I could touch it once the road was done. And suddenly, I stopped and looked around me. Thousands of monotone people stared at me, anxious to see what my next move would be. That's when I noticed I was completely naked too, but it was as if my insecurities had disappeared in a split second. As I took another step, the people bowed towards me on the floor and recited some *words in an unrecognizable language. As I walked along further, I could hear Albert lure me further, but with no knowledge of his location. I quickly began to feel a sudden adoration from the people around me that made me smile widely and enjoy the moment more than I would admit.*

*That's when I woke up.*

*I've been thinking a lot about this dream. I had heard whispers in the house before about the strange dreams that The Path induced on Albert, which he indeed referred to as visions, but I doubted I was having one myself. After all, it would only make me the second practitioner to experience them after Mr. Kaine, and I seriously pondered whether that was even possible. Nevertheless, I decided to keep it to myself; maybe it helps as a test to keep it to myself and concentrate on my path.*

*I've also been thinking about the meaning behind it. It certainly looked apocalyptic to me, and that is what Albert says is the end of all of our paths if we aren't successful in our mission. That raises a serious question: if my dream were to be a vision indeed, is it telling me our purpose fails? Albert has always said to us that we have to beware sometimes of* what The Path shows us, as nothing ever really is set in stone, and it's just merely a possibility in the vast field of possible outcomes. But at the very least, it could be telling me we aren't working hard enough.

Am I looking too hard into it? I'm not quite sure. Maybe I am. Or perhaps that is the way it all ends. But why was I at the center of everything? Am I the key to something bigger? Albert previously told me that answers manifest itself as light, so could the literal light I was approaching be the answer we have been searching for? But why was I the one to contact it on the dream and not him?

**What is my role in all of this?**

# 6

We stayed in Green River for two weeks. While the town wasn't anything to write home about except for the beautiful nature, I remember the time fondly, probably because it was one of the last times before everything went downhill.

Despite my initial faith and devotion to The Path, I was beginning to have some questions that I doubted Albert held the answers too. After my mysterious dream, I found myself repeatedly thinking about it but reluctant to tell it to him.

Regardless of my evident admiration for him, there was still a precise reason I couldn't directly point to that was holding my trust for him back. I did, however, tell it to Lee, who had become a great friend of mine during the trip, especially after a contentious moment we shared when he had a nervous breakdown at night. I felt a substantial emotional connection to him I hadn't sensed for a friend for a long time, which was a delightful surprise. Once I told him all about my dream, he too advised me not to tell Albert, citing his discomfort with some past comments made to him in a therapy he wasn't willing to disclose to me, but I trusted him. Kaine unquestionably was the type of person who would command some sense of intimidation even in friendly environments, so I completely understood where Lee's skepticism about Albert came from. I instead decided to write my dream down in detail and save it for any possible occasion where it might be helpful.

A few days after we arrived back home, I was notified of the next trip: a visit to Los Angeles to meet with a radio host who would book Albert for a quick appearance. It would be an even greater distance trip, but after seeing my daughter enjoying her time at the Kaine house with the incoming members of The Path, I was confident enough to leave her there a few more days.

Notwithstanding my increasing suspicion of Albert's intentions, I had no clear evidence to back it up, which accordingly made me look forward to the trip to possibly rekindle our relationship. What indeed didn't help were the last few sessions of therapy, where I had felt Albert was becoming increasingly personal in his questionings. In a particular moment of tension, he had questioned my love for my wife, which he doubted was real because of me mentioning my deep admiration for her sister, something he noted could be a sign of my unfaithfulness for her. It irritated me, perhaps because the argument wasn't entirely based in fiction: I did indeed have an affair with Lori's sister, only her other one. Nevertheless, his words were too harsh for me to bear and to cope with. I felt guilty. As soon as some days passed, I looked deep inside of me. I realized that I had to deal with that side of me to continue my Path. Maybe I had to trust Albert. That is what motivated me to anticipate the trip to Los Angeles, where I planned on finally telling him about my dream.

# 7

I want to go back, Lori. Back to where I once was happy. I want to come back home from work and see you there with that smile of yours I never seem to forget. To taste your delicious pasta. To accidentally fall asleep beside you and wake up looking at your tender face sleeping. To smell that perfume you never seemed to get tired off. I get the impression everything would be different with you here. We never got to do so many things we planned, and yet, I wouldn't change a thing we did together. I always go back to that moment I decided to talk to you and catch myself smiling with a tear falling down my cheek because I realize it was the best decision I could have ever made. I sometimes wish so hard you were here that I believe it, and I call you only to hear your sweet voice remind me you're not here by telling me to leave a message.

I wish I would have never let you go that day. We were going through a rough time, but I never stopped loving you, but I'm scared that you left without never knowing it.

I made big mistakes, but none as hurtful as letting you go that day. To hear myself choke

up when I heard you were gone was the hardest part, yet I think I never have fully coped with it.

I miss you, Lori. I just wish you knew.

# 8

*Hello again. It's been a while since I have written here. It's strange because every time I end up writing, I enjoy it quite a bit, but I just never find the time to do it. It's also been a strange dilemma for me because I've often wondered who will end up reading this journal. I mean, unless I get rid of it, I believe someone must find it eventually and read it despite my best intentions to keep it personal. It was an uncomfortable idea at the time, but now I kind of like it as it keeps things more interesting, although I just wish I could know more about you, too. How is the world at the moment you're living in? Is it post-apocalyptic? If my vision ends up being true, I'm going to be alive when everything ends, so I guess you couldn't be reading this before that event.*

*Unless I lost it?...*

*Haha. Back to journaling!*

*We have been in LA for three days, and I have to say that I've appreciated the time I've spent with Albert. I genuinely feel like I'm getting to know a more human side of him I've never fully gotten the chance to appreciate in our daily interactions. He has told me a lot about his childhood and how he has dealt with some tragedies with his own, like when he lost his grandparents at an early age and how he lived in extreme poverty. I find myself often wondering again what his exact age is. I can't shake off the feeling that I am talking to an old man when having conversations with him, but I doubt he's a year over fifty.*

*On the first day, we visited Hillary, an old acquaintance of Albert, who had some connections in the entertainment world. She had a brief conversation with me, where she told me how she had breast cancer, and Albert helped her heal. She refused to go into detail about what he did to cure her, but she said that ever since that moment she has wholly committed herself to the teachings of The Path. Albert told me he loved her story, although he too refused to say to me exactly how he led her to her cure. Strange. That specific moment suddenly reminded me why I still have some mixed feelings about him. Why wouldn't they reveal it? I am a staunch defender and practitioner of The Path, but even I had to pause and think about what the possibility was of such a thing happening.*

*Nevertheless, I had to ignore my doubts to continue on our mission to get Albert on the radio, and the next day, we achieved it. He was booked on a morning radio show that explored daily news and was featured in a segment regarding alternative medicine and practices that were growing in prominence. And he truly did shine on it; in fact, I was amazed at his incredible skill of communicating The Path to the world. I'm not entirely sure yet, but there's something about him that truly captivates everyone around him. It's a certain warmth, I'd say, that you seldom see in your life, perhaps something akin to parental affection. Maybe that's what reminded me of a grandpa when I spoke with him. Tonight, we are going to a bar. I'm planning on finally telling him about my dream.*

# 9

Albert and I sat on a small round table in the bar when I finally had the guts to tell him about my dream. I knew him to be a highly unpredictable character, so I never really expected a specific reaction from him. I had the urge to tell him more so as I felt it was my responsibility as a lower practitioner to let him know what I had seen.

I began to tell him the dream in detail nervously; the rocky road, my feet bleeding, my naked body, my beard, the bright sun, the people worshiping me, his voice. He listened but never saw me directly in the eyes. At times, I even wondered if he was thinking of something else. As I finished, he finally looked up. His eyes were filled with tears.

"That was beautiful, son," he said, as he broke down in tears. "I need you to write this down in detail. Now, excuse me, but I need to leave. I'm sorry."

And he did. He left the bar with a red face as he tried to hold back tears, and we never spoke about it again. I still wonder what was so emotional about it to him, but it made me think that it might have had a deeper meaning than I had previously anticipated.

I couldn't deny that despite my happiness that he had seemingly gotten some meaning out of my dream, there was something inside me that rattled me. As I thought long and hard about our interaction that night, my initial thoughts evolved from him being truly in awe of my dream to him being disturbed by it. I couldn't explain it, but from that day onward, I felt a strange, uneasy feeling about Albert and The Path. There was something that unsettled me. It was a combination of several things. I still felt very bothered by the idea that he found me out of nowhere and ended up convincing me of this made-up philosophy. I found Lee's feelings about him strangely, not far-fetched. How did he cure Hillary of cancer? Despite all of the stories he's told me about his life, there was still a strange sensation when I heard them. Something wasn't adding up.

As we left LA, I couldn't stop thinking about all of this. I didn't feel as committed to The Path as before. From that point, everything changed.

# PART TWO

# 10

After days of being away, we arrived at home. I expected the house to be as we left it, but it was far from that: it had been painted outside with a pastel pink color and remodeled from the inside. Albert told me it was the work of some Lieutenant Preceptors who had tasked themselves with adorning the house as faithful to The Path as possible. Upon Albert's recommendation, they mostly left behind the color white as he considered it "too plain and not at all indicative of the ideals of The Path."

The members received us with an incredible party. It was stuffed with snacks and a delicious turkey made by Linda, a newcomer to The Path. The house was filling up faster than ever before, as at least twenty new members were living in it.

"We might soon need to move," Albert told me in the middle of the party, as he continued to enjoy the festivity.

I was told my daughter was in the middle of a teaching lesson. The one person I couldn't find, however, was Lee, who had mysteriously been absent from the party and was nowhere to be found. When I asked around, they all said the same thing: he was out grocery shopping with other preceptors. Still, it was hard for me to believe it since I didn't find anyone else who was missing but him, and the only logical conclusion would be to assume that he left with newcomers I had yet to meet, but it still rubbed me the wrong way.

After a long day, I went to sleep, tired, and without taking my daily therapy, realizing it was probably for the best since most were under the influence. It also would help me to analyze my growing thoughts regarding The Path further.

I was no longer sure about my belief in The Path. If it weren't for my dream, I would abandon the ideology completely, but that was still holding me back. My more optimistic and idealistic side told me that it was probably part of my process to have doubts at the beginning, and to give up wouldn't be worth it. Perhaps it was true. But I still thought about the uneasy feeling I had. If my sentiments towards The Path and Albert Kaine were only an ideological phase and nothing more, it would be easier to quit.

However, it was my connection to Albert, even if I doubted his intentions, which prevented me from ever leaving him behind. Besides, what made me so sure that what he preached wasn't real? He had cured my of my addiction to alcohol, and I was mostly freed from depression aside from some occasional episodes, and my dream had to mean something. Maybe I just needed some more clarity to make me walk further along The Path. Still, hard to ignore everything that made me doubt it in the first place.

I keep going back to my initial question: how did he find me? He claims to be continually looking for people like me, and he happened to stumble upon me, but it just doesn't ring true to me.

That's when my anxiety regarding Lee came back to me. There had to be a reason he wasn't at the party. I never saw him again.

I left the room quietly. Everyone was asleep. I swiftly approached Lee's bedroom, but it was locked. That calmed me: he was probably back and asleep. As I went back to my room, I felt a warm presence behind me.

"Is there a problem, Roy?" Albert asked me as I nervously turned around to face him.

I sighed. "I was looking for Lee. It turns out he's asleep. I'm going back to bed."

"I have sensed something strange about you, Roy. Something isn't right about you since we came back. I hope everything is well."

Maybe I was too obvious. "No, everything is fine, Albert. Really. I'm as committed as ever to The Path. I guess I've just been remembering Lori lately."

He remained still, let out a soft, intimidating smile, and then left. I went into my room. I found myself sweating uncontrollably.

I could now say, with complete certainty, that I was becoming afraid of Albert Kaine.

# 11

The next day, Albert had been preparing with some other Lieutenant Preceptors a luncheon to formally celebrate the newcomers to The Path and share some news. It was there that I became confident Lee had disappeared. There was no space in the table for him, and there wasn't even a mere mention of his name. However, I was also getting the impression that something had been done to him. The fake joyous nature of the gathering made me furious, but I decided to contain my emotions as I had realized that publicly pointing out Lee's absence wouldn't be in my best interest.

The luncheon was a regular meeting for Albert, who would usually fall into the same talking points about The Path and the work we had to do as a community to continue our mission forward. The adoration for him slightly amused me, even while fully realizing that I was part of that sentiment before.

Before it ended, I silently left and went into Lee's room, which was now unlocked, only to find another man sleeping inside. That's when the alarm bells in my head indeed went off. Was I living in a cult? Was leaving still a choice for me?

As I pondered on these questions, Albert ordered me to his office. He was cold and uninviting, as if the man I had known before had begun to reveal himself to me. He signaled me to sit down.

"I think we should continue our conversation from last night," he blurted as if an accusation was on its way.

"What's to continue, Albert?"

"I truly think there's something wrong with you, Roy."

"Everything is fine. Really. I'm fine."

"Yesterday, you said you were as committed as ever to The

Path. But I didn't even question that. Why was that?"

"I must have mistaken your question yesterday. I thought maybe you doubted my commitment to you. I wanted to assure

you that I wasn't wavering."

He chuckled. "And yet, you felt the urge to assure me of that."

He came closer to me and whispered in my ear. "What were you doing last night?"

"I told you, I was looking for Lee. I didn't see him. Figured he was sleeping."

The tension-filled conversation was heating up. I was ready to confront him, even if my brain said otherwise.

"Although I didn't see him at the luncheon either. I was going to ask you, Albert, if you had any knowledge of his whereabouts. I wouldn't want to feel he has disappeared —"

"Is that a threat?"

What? "What? No, Albert, I think you're getting everything wrong."

I stood up from the chair and backed away a bit.

"Look, I'm genuinely worried about Lee. That is all. That's the truth. I should have been upfront about it from the beginning, yes, but I was nervous, okay? I just need to know he's fine."

"What makes you nervous?"

I felt a sudden rush of emotion overtake me. "Nothing. I don't know. I'm not sure."

"You know Roy, you keep assuring me you're committed to The Path and its cause, yet you suddenly come filled with accusations and, all of a sudden, you're nervous and emotional talking to me. I'm getting the complete opposite conclusion from you than what you are telling me."

I wasn't liking the exchange, and to make matters worse, he had no answers regarding Lee.

"Albert, please. I'm invested in The Path. I just need to find Lee. I need to find Lee, and then I can leave with my daughter if that's your wish."

That last sentence raised his eyebrows. He wasn't expecting me to suggest I was planning on leaving.

He once again came closer to me.

"No. You're not leaving with anyone. Your daughter is happier than she has ever been before here. As opposed to you, she has committed, Roy. Maybe you need a lesson to pull yourself back up. I'll give you a month to think about it."

I barely had time to adequately react to his comment before I felt a strong man forcefully grabbing me from behind.

I was thrown and locked inside a small, dark room.

# 12

I'm not sure what the date is anymore. Now it has been a long time. They didn't take the time to check what I had with me, so at least I have you to keep me company this month. I can only write during the day when a thin ray of sunshine comes through the hole where they throw me food.

I wish I could take it all back. I wish I had never spoken about Lee. Hell, I wish I had never even accepted to join this shit from the beginning. What did I get myself into? What did I do to deserve this? Now my daughter is trapped with them without knowing the evil that lurks inside. I would have preferred to kill myself with booze than to have ever come here.

If I hadn't let Lori leave that day, I wouldn't be lying on the ground here; we would be watching TV and eating Chinese food as if nothing had ever happened. I completely fucked up.

*And now I have no plan. When I get out of here, how can I leave? I've thought about killing Albert. But what would that solve? What the hell happened to Lee? I probably need to find that out first if I ever want to leave.*

*What if Lee is in one of these rooms too? It would make sense. He told me he didn't trust Albert. Maybe the had a confrontation that ended up in him being locked inside one as well. Maybe when I leave, he's already out. Poor Lee.*

# 13

I'm not even counting the number of entries this has

*i miss you Lori*

*What can i do to have you back?*

*I've been thinking about killing myself with paper cuts from this journal.*

*or maybe I can break the toilet without making any noise and kill myself with a piece*

*im becoming weak. i cant write correctly or for too long. im tired.*

*My eyes can barely stay open*

*im going to kill albert when i get out*

# 14

*no*

*i need to keep him alive*

**obey him**

*be faithful to the path again*

# 15

*dreaming again about killing him again*

*i try not to*

*what can i do lori*

*help me lori*

# 16

*no killing*

*keep him alive*

*obey mr Kaine*

*find Lee*

*then escape*

**escape**

# 17

After a long, depressing month, I saw a towering figure open the door. The light could barely let me adjust my eyes to precisely decipher who it was. He grabbed me. I was as thin and small as a toddler. I could barely move without feeling fragile. The man suddenly dropped me in a warm bathtub, and my eyes finally could recognize him: Albert.

"You did good, Roy," he muttered. "Did I?"

"Yes, you did."

"Where's my daughter?"

"I'll let you change first. Then I'll come for you."

I stayed in the tub for over an hour. You never fully appreciate cleaning yourself until you've spent over a month without it. My skin felt as soft as a fish, and the clothes felt as comfortable as anything I had worn before. As promised, Albert came for me when I was done. He walked me towards the garden.

"Look there, Roy."

He pointed out with his finger to a couple playing with my daughter. She seemed happier than ever.

"She was desperate to find some sense of belonging. You were gone for far too long. She's been delighted with them."

I could see it. I could never make her that happy ever since Lori left.

That's when I reconsidered. Maybe this was right. Perhaps, as I had once thought, this was all part of my therapy, and my daughter being truly happy required me to be away.

"I could never give her that, Albert."

"Don't be so hard on yourself. She still loves you. You just need to let go. It's for the best."

"Yes. You're right. It's part of my Path," I admitted. "I need you to forgive me, Albert. For everything. I'm ready to get back into The Path for good."

Albert smiled. "I knew you'd be back."

Even while saying it, I was unsure of what my true feelings were now that I was back outside. I sincerely did wish to get better and understood that my daughter was happier where she was, but the thought of Lee still haunted me. Perhaps it was best to move on.

# 18

The Path was getting bigger faster than I had anticipated. From the time I was locked in that room to when I got outside, at least thirty new members arrived; Albert cited the radio interview as the cause of the expansion. He also told me the community was growing in other parts of the world. By the time Christmas came, we had already moved to a bigger house, and the community had been separated into two groups. I joined the new home with Albert.

For the first time in quite a few years, I didn't celebrate Christmas Eve, as Albert opposed the idea due to the conflicting ideological dilemma it would impose. It was a strange reason given that he had always told me to separate The Path from a religious denomination. It was around Christmas and New Year's Eve when he told me we would be traveling at the beginning of January to Tallahassee for a convention where he would speak directly to a crowd of hundredths of interested students.

While I was skeptical about getting too excited about the trip, I was at the very least mildly looking forward to it, if even just to have a chance at easing my relationship once again with him. My plan was clear. I would accompany Albert on this last trip and try and get on his good side, and there I would make a decision: either to stay indefinitely and once again pledge my loyalty to The Path or request to leave, something that I wasn't quite sure would be possible.

It was also around this time that, with Albert's encouragement, I began writing letters to my daughter. Even though she wasn't authorized to respond, I felt safe having the option of communication with her open to me.

I was still too skeptical to consider me back into The Path officially, but at the very least, the feeling of steadiness made me feel at ease, especially following a rough month.

Even if my situation wasn't ideal, I was lucky to have everything I needed to live, and basically, a family as well. Families fight, right? I would think, as I would try to leave behind my past differences with Albert. But even as I felt a slight desire to fall back on him, I couldn't forget about Lee. It was almost as if he had been a mere illusion, one that was there one day, but the next one was completely gone with no trace left. He was the main reason I was holding myself back from embracing The Path again.

# 19

I've always been fascinated by the concept of "truth." Isn't it funny that we get so wrapped up in it sometimes that we lose sight of the fact that there is no singular objective truth to anything? Even what I'm laying out right now as an idea in my head is just true for me – but maybe it isn't to you.

Funny.

Maybe.

Some days, these kinds of thoughts can entertain me for hours,

not because I want to, but because I have no choice. I guess I'm becoming used to it.

To be completely honest, I'm honestly still not sure why I have been writing all of this. In the beginning, I thought it would be a helpful physical record in case the truth would be twisted against me, but now I'm not even sure what I will do. Maybe I just wrote all of this because I've always wanted to be a writer, so it served as an excuse. But I need to be careful. I have ripped some pages from my original journal here that could serve as a further context to what has happened, and in its place, I've been writing in it tirelessly in case someone finds it. What will they stumble upon if they indeed find it? A bunch of fairytale stories of how I've learned to love The Path; it's hilarious even to put it that way. I've learned far too much to trust Albert even an ounce, so I'd rather be extra careful with every action I take.

I'm near the end, anyway. So I might as well finish the story before I make a move.

# 20

Soon after the holidays were over, it was time for Tallahassee. After an unexpected flush of new activities to be done, Albert decided to split the groups into two, where he would work during the trip with some Lieutenant Preceptors on one car, and I would travel with his wife, Amy. I had heard before about Amy, but I had never had the chance to meet her adequately. I suspected Albert wasn't the best husband to have, but of course, I never questioned their relationship. Lee and I had once noticed it was a fragile topic to bring up in front of him.

The car smelled like pumpkin spice. It was, overall, a nice time to be around her. In a way, it was the first real interactions I had with a "normal" person in quite a while, as Amy barely mentioned Albert or The Path. I speculated, possibly correctly, that she wasn't fond of either.

In some ways, she reminded me of Lori, which could explain the instant connection I felt to her. She was everything Albert wasn't, so I could, at the very least, understand why they once fell for each other.

When we arrived, we immediately headed to the hotel Albert had booked, who mysteriously had placed everyone in separate rooms, including his wife.

As soon as we had arrived, I was already sensing something peculiar about Albert. He was sweating much more than usual, he could barely finish a conversation before he had to go to the restroom, his shave wasn't great, and he repeatedly isolated himself. So, to the surprise of no one, he became ill, and he had to task the Lieutenant Preceptors to speak on behalf of him at the convention as Amy and I were to stay and take care of him. As the usual stubborn goat he is, he refused to go to a hospital, insisting The Path would show him a way to heal. Once again, I found myself losing my nerve to Albert.

In a certain way, I have to admit that I slightly enjoyed looking at him that way. He looked weak, almost too weak, and he suddenly had lost all of his charm. It was therapeutic to see him inferiorly, even as I felt wrong about thinking it.

And yet, to my surprise, it wasn't the greatest enjoyment I got out of that day: that was spending time with Amy. And yes, being fully aware of the potential penalty that could obtain me within The Path, I just couldn't help but feel attracted to her. There was a particular type of tension between us that would later be confirmed that night. I have to admit that even knowing the full extent of what mingling with her could mean to me, I didn't care enough to stop.

Much of my reasoning behind staying, as I stated before, was due to the steadiness I couldn't afford anywhere else – and for that, I was indeed thankful to Albert. Still, spending time with Amy made me realize that it was exactly just that, not a potential reawakening to The Path. Perhaps I was never as engaged with it as I thought. Still, instead of at least having the urge to practice it, my contentious relationship with Albert had wiped that away.

And so, as I expected, that night ended with the wife of a man I once admired in my bed. And I loved every second with it. To be fully transparent, the sparse guilt I felt for falling for her disappeared as we were together at night.

# 21

The sun in my face woke me up in the morning. Amy was gone.

I quickly changed. I barely had left the room to look for her when I saw Albert standing in the hallway. He wasn't losing time. "I'm feeling like a new car this morning. There's no time to waste. Let's get some breakfast. I need to talk to you. I'll meet you

in the lobby?"

He needed to speak with me. It was there when I could see the

writing on the wall: he must have seen me with Amy. He must have. There was not a single step that I took towards the lobby without thinking of a million excuses. How do you spin fucking someone's wife? I thought about running away, escaping. But that wouldn't be good. No. I had to beg for forgiveness. My daughter was still in the house. Getting abandoned in Tallahassee wasn't part of my plan. No. I would deny it ever happened, blame Amy, send a letter to my daughter, set a meeting place at home, and escape. That was the only way.

I saw him desperately eating a chocolate donut in a table for two. I joined him. I was sweating embarrassingly. I felt like a kid facing the principal.

"Albert I–"

"Sorry, Roy, but I'll get the first word. No time to waste, okay?" he babbled. "The Path was trying to show me something, Roy. That's what made me sick yesterday. I knew something was up. But you need to hear this."

I felt as if a huge weight had been lifted off from me. He wouldn't question me about Amy. He came closer and began whispering.

"I had a vision last night, Roy. A big one. Bigger than any other I've had. I saw the end of time. But not like other times, no. I found the true purpose of The Path. All this time, I've – we've – had it wrong. I spent all this time thinking The Path existed to stop the end of the world, to prevent it from ever happening by way of healing as many souls as possible. But it was false. I never saw it correctly. My Path is to heal these souls not to save the world, but to survive it, Roy. Only true believers of The Path will survive. It was right in front of me all this time. And it makes sense. We can't prevent a certain event, but we can prevent a personal fate. This changes everything."

His eyes were watery. I could tell he had never been more excited than by this discovery. But was it sincere?

"Roy, think about it. You had your dream. In your vision, you heard me guiding you. You saw other Path-seekers adoring you. And it was already after the apocalypse. At the time, it never connected with me, but now it makes perfect sense: we are meant to survive, and I think you will succeed me. I believe I may not survive for some reason, and you'll take my mantle."

The information came too fast for me to process at the moment. Despite my all-but abandonment for The Path, for some odd reason, Albert's new vision didn't ring entirely false for me. Perhaps it was because of my own. It all made sense when pieced together.

He looked attentively at me.

"This changes everything, son. Everything. We leave tonight. I need to do some writings right now. But I'll see you here in the afternoon."

As hard as I tried, I couldn't hold back my curiosity.

"Albert, where's Amy? I haven't seen her today."

His face immediately turned red, and his smile disappeared. "What do you mean?"

"Yes, I mean, we were taking care of you last night, and I haven't seen her. I was just curious."

He was taken aback by the question.

"Oh. She left this morning with the other preceptors. She wanted to go home. Don't worry about it, Roy."


He swiftly left the table and walked rapidly to his room.

# 22

I don't have much time to finish writing this.

Long story short, after my conversation with Albert, I came directly to my room and began writing all of this. I've made up my mind: I need to get the hell away from Albert. I need my daughter back, gather my things, and leave. I have no alternative. This has been too much.

Visions and end of the world conversations are not how I planned on spending the rest of my life. Either Albert and his preceptors are a bunch of crazies, or they're the key to surviving humanity in the impending doom. Yes, I choose to believe the former for now.

This is the end. Now it's time to plot my escape.

# PART THREE

# 23

*Honey, it's daddy. I know I haven't been there for you that much since we arrived here, but I will make it up to you. The thing is, I have now realized that it is in our best interest to leave. I have been led to believe lies and to practice a philosophy I consider to be faulty at best. I sincerely hope you understand.*

*I love you.*

*Mommy loved you.*

*I'm so sorry.*

*Meet me on Tuesday at the entrance. Mr. Kaine is planning on making an announcement. That will be our moment to escape. I sincerely expect you to understand.*

*-Dad*

•••

It's time to go; Albert is already waiting for me outside. I have my plan wholly set up: we will arrive tomorrow morning at home, where we will pass through the old house to pick up some of Albert's stuff. That will be my moment to sneak the letter into her room. Then, it's just a matter of trusting her and waiting for Tuesday. *Nothing could go wrong, right?*

# 24

Well, everything is going like planned for now.

Just as I had expected, we passed through the old home. It was slightly more challenging to find her room given the reorganization of the house, but I managed to do it on time. I just hope she follows the plan.

What bothers me the most is that I will most likely have to leave with no answers. How did Albert exactly find me? Where's Lee? Where's Amy?

Albert keeps reassuring me that Amy is a dedicated introvert, and she's at home, yet I still find it confounding to not yet hear from her since the trip. I mean, not a single word, at least in private, about our night together? She must have something to say.

Unless Albert did find out.

But how would he? I seriously doubt she would confess it to him, especially considering how good he's been treating me since Tallahassee. To be honest, this whole thing has felt like a twisted dream since I got out of that small dark room. Nothing feels real. I sometimes feel like I'm hallucinating.

Albert can't stop talking about his new vision with me. At least I have to give him credit, he's very passionate about The Path. There was, admittedly, a time where I believed he could be faking it, but now I don't think that's true. I think he genuinely believes in this shit, and he also happens to be a good persuader. Without being one, I probably wouldn't have ever even considered joining him. Yet, this is where I find myself.

Could I press charges against him? Would it be worth it? I'm still not sure what my actions should be after leaving this place. Even more so, I can't even picture myself outside: an illegally functioning cult has thoroughly institutionalized me. I guess that says a lot about the state of mind I found myself when he took me in.

If I had to list positives of my experience here honestly, it would be that I have been woken up, not by "finding my Path" or any of that bullshit, but by getting back to my senses. I genuinely haven't felt more awoken since Lori died.

# 25

# TUESDAY

Today is finally the day. I'm ready. I can feel the adrenaline trying to overtake me. But I need to hang on. For Lori.

Have you ever felt so willing to abandon something, and just around the time you're about to do it, you start to question your judgment? That's exactly how I feel right now. I'm not sure this is the correct thing to do. Not even morally. Am I really willing to abandon this place without having the answers I've been craving for? I'm scared they will haunt me forever if I leave now.

But I have no time.

The house is filled with guests, some which I have never even seen. Has The Path grown this big in the few days I wasn't here?

They're all formally dressed. I should have worn something more suited for the occasion; I look like a bum among these people.

In a matter of minutes, my daughter supposed to meet me at the entrance.

Fuck.

Albert is walking towards me.

"Roy!" he screams. "Roy. This will be the moment for me to tell them about my vision. Today everything changes. I'm so glad to have you by my side for this, truly. I need you to join me in the end."

Just what I needed.

"Sure, Albert, no problem. I'll be down here waiting for your call."

"Thank you, Roy. Honestly, from the heart. Thank you."

He's emotional. I know how much this means to him. Nevertheless, I need to leave now.

I walk towards the entrance, watching over my shoulder through every step I take. The guests are gathering around him. He watches over them, standing on a small stage in the garden.

I sneak through the small hallway towards the entrance. No one is here. Good, this might be easier than I previously thought.

She's not here yet. She's probably finding her way to sneak out from the gathering too.

I can hear Roy speaking to the people from here.

"My fellow path-seekers, my preceptors...I have some news this morning that may cause some uproar. As you all well know, I was in Florida some days back. It was a nice trip, but I fell ill for most of it. But my people, it wasn't just a normal sickness. I had a vision. A nightmarish vision, mind you: I've seen our true Path. For all of us. Everything has changed."

She's not here.

"You see, The Path...we are meant to be survivors, not saviors. That might sound like a downgrade to some of you, but you need to understand that to survive what is coming will be the biggest superpower one can have in the New World that The Path has laid out for me."

She's still not here.

I'm trying to block out evil thoughts, but I can't. Could this be? Could she have gone missing too? Oh, no. Fuck. Fuck.

How could I not see it coming?

"...I want to introduce my partner in all this, and my successor in many ways: Roy Hill."

The crowd has erupted in applause. I can barely hear them. Everything has been drowned out by my mind.

I'm not thinking straight.

What did I get myself into?

I can't help it. I feel like a machine without control. I'm walking towards him. These are tears of anger, not of sadness. I grab the knife beside the cake. I'm not thinking orderly.

"Where's my daughter Albert."

The cheers have transformed into a silent horror. Albert steps back.

"Roy. Listen to me. Your daughter has not been feeling well. She decided not to come today–"

"Where's Amy? Where's your wife, Roy?"

I can see the confusion in everyone else's faces. I continue.

"Yes, for those of you not aware, Albert has a wife. A wife he doesn't show. She has gone missing. Where is she? Where is Lee Albert?"

"I need you to calm down, Roy."

"I'm not going to fucking calm down until you tell me where they are. This is a cult. I don't even know how I ever listened to you."

"You want to know where she is? Fine. See for yourself."

He points to her room. I walk towards it, slowly. I can feel my hand trembling, but not enough to drop the knife. I carefully open the door.

There is no one in the room.

Albert comes closer to me. He grabs my hand. I'm sobbing.

"Roy. You're not thinking straight. I should've known this would happen. I thought you would find the truth within yourself, but now I realize I should've said it to you earlier."

My mind has gone blank. What does he mean?

"Think about it. Think about everything. Your wife. Your daughter. Lee. Amy. Think about everything you've been through since you arrived. Does anything not quite fit in the story?"

What does he mean?

"When you needed familiarity, your daughter was there. When you needed friendship, Lee was there. When you needed passion,

Amy was there. But once you fulfilled every desire, they were gone from your life. Why is that Roy? Think long and hard about it."

No.

No.

*That can't be.*

No.

*Oh my god.*

Yes.

**It's true.**

Lori was pregnant when she died.

We never had the time to name her, but we only knew she was a girl.

*I never had a daughter.*

*Lee wasn't real.*

*Amy wasn't either.*

"I decided to go along with it sometimes to study you further. But I now realize it was a mistake Roy, and for that, I am truly sorry."

I am in disbelief. I finally open my mouth.

"But...I had sex with Amy, Albert. I did."

"Can't you remember that she died as well? That's what made us bond in the first place, Roy. Look inside your brain. Can you recall?"

Yes. I can recall. *He's right. He did tell me.* I just willingly chose to erase it from my brain. *What is wrong with me?*

"I realized you were special since you came here because I was never looking for you. I think you summoned a person who gave you directions, and you wound up here. But the funny thing is, you found the place by yourself. The Path was shown to you by a literal person made up in your mind who guided you to where you're standing now. They all manifested as needs to serve as obstacles for your true awakening. I now realize it, after both our visions, that you're a messiah of the cause."

Is this true? Has this all been part of my awakening?

"Roy, but there's something else. Something far more peculiar that made the situation even more special in my eyes. But I need you to calm down before you hear this."

I can sense a gut punch coming.

"I was the one who crashed with your wife. I'm the cause of her death, Roy. And I believe that you coming to me was part of my awakening too. I needed to cope with that."

Oh, I have awakened all right.

Not only have I been living a lie for the past year, but I've been willingly working for my wife's killer.

I can't help it.

*Stop.*


**Stop.**


In a split second, I catch myself stabbing Albert in the chest. Blood quickly fills it up. I'm shocked at my actions, but he isn't.

He grabs the knife from his chest as tears fill up his body. The gathered guests begin to smile. Were they expecting this? Albert leads me to the stage.

Everything is blurry now. Have I been led by The Path this whole time?

As I get up on the stage, more people arrive, as they chant in a language I can't decipher.

Is this what adoration feels like? Has this been what I've been looking for all this time?

Despite Albert's growing bloodstain and his pale face, he's fully embracing me. I think he's proud of me. Even as my brain tells me to avoid it, I can't help but succumb to their ritual.

### *Do I believe in The Path?*

Every valuable piece of information is flashing in front of me: the car crash, the police officer, my daughter, Lee, Amy. Were they all a product of my imagination? But if they were, wouldn't there be a hole in my story? Have I trusted Albert once again and blinded my perception of what truly happened, or is he right?

And yet, I remember my vision too. Maybe The Path was indeed showing me my true fate. Albert was dead in that vision, and he's dying right in front of me. Perhaps everything is indeed going as planned. I remember that vision so vividly that I almost feel like I lived it.

But within flashes of my vision, I also see Lee and Amy's corpses. What if he is lying to me, and I'm abandoning their only hope of someone finding them?

Has The Path truly awakened me, or put me to sleep?

The reverence I'm feeling is clouding my thoughts, but I can't help it.

*Maybe I'm right where I'm supposed to be.*

www.ingramcontent.com/pod-product-compliance
Lightning Source LLC
Chambersburg PA
CBHW020918180626

46816CB00007BA/2463

* 9 7 8 1 6 7 8 1 8 3 4 5 5 *